To the memory of my mother, Irene McPike
—E.McP.

For Brett, with love
—P.B.

G. P. Putnam's Sons
Published by the Penguin Group
Penguin Group (USA) LLC
375 Hudson Street
New York, NY 10014

USA | Canada | UK | Ireland | Australia
New Zealand | India | South Africa | China
penguin.com
A Penguin Random House Company

Library of Congress Cataloging-in-Publication Data
McPike, Elizabeth.
Little sleepyhead / Elizabeth McPike ; illustrated by Patrice Barton.
pages cm
Summary: "After a busy day filled with loved ones, adventure, and fun, baby is tired from head to toe"—Provided by publisher.
[1. Stories in rhyme. 2. Bedtime—Fiction. 3. Babies—Fiction.] I. Barton, Patrice, 1955- illustrator. II. Title.
PZ8.3.M46175Lit 2015
[E]—dc23
2013040027

Manufactured in China.
ISBN 978-0-399-16240-4
3 5 7 9 10 8 6 4
Special Markets ISBN 978-0-399-54580-1 Not for Resale

Design by Marikka Tamura. Text set in Cooper OldStyle Demi.
The images were created using pencil sketches and mixed media that were assembled and painted digitally.

This Imagination Library edition is published by Penguin Young Readers, a division
of Penguin Random House, exclusively for Dolly Parton's Imagination Library,
a not-for-profit program designed to inspire a love of reading and learning, sponsored
in part by The Dollywood Foundation. Penguin's trade editions of this work are
available wherever books are sold.

Little Sleepyhead

Elizabeth McPike · Patrice Barton

G. P. Putnam's Sons
An Imprint of Penguin Group (USA)

Tired little toes,
wiggling one to ten,

Tired little feet,
think of where they've been.

Tired little knees,
crawling to and from,

Tired little tummy,
full of yum, yum, yum.

Tired little arms,
stretching up so high,

Tired little hands,
waving bye, bye, bye.

Tired little neck,
bending back to see,

Tired little ears,
listening do, re, mi.

Tired little lips,
blowing kisses sweet,

Tired little heart,
never skips a beat.

Tired little eyes,
ready now for bed,

Tired little everything,
precious sleepyhead.

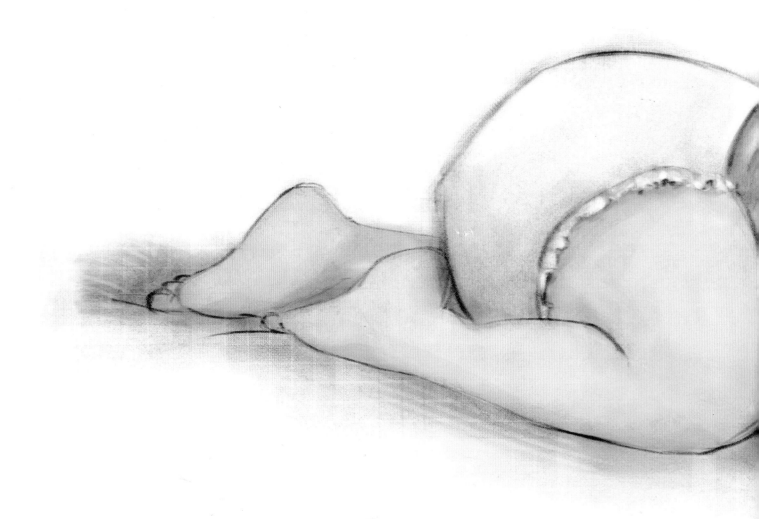

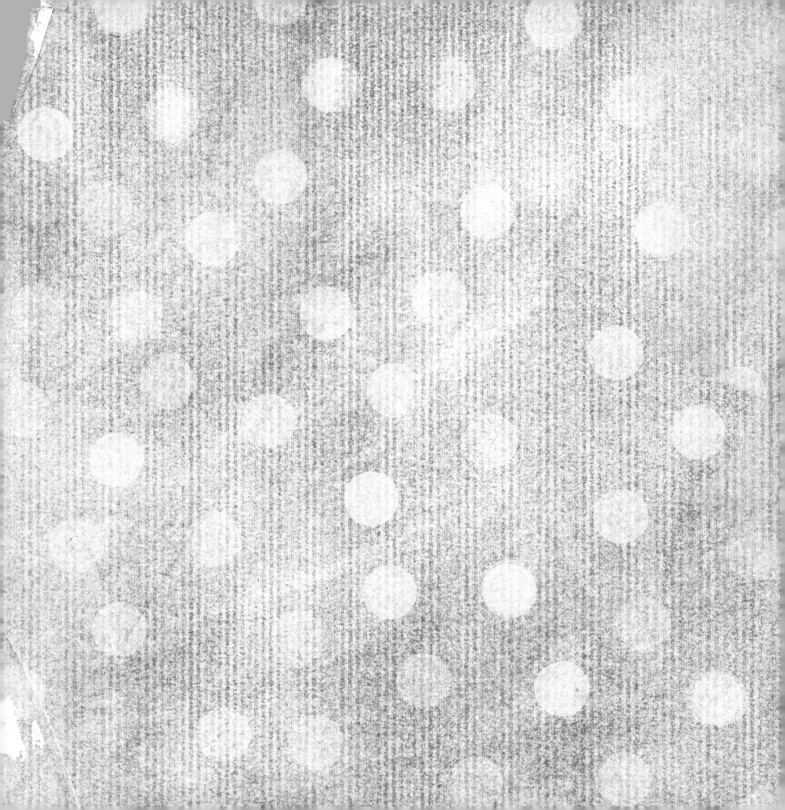